Family
Reminders

D0954618

Family Reminders

Julie Danneberg

Illustrated by John Shelley

ꕹ Charlesbridge

To Walker, Alex, and Jack,
as we continue to make our own family memories
—J. D.

For Sophie, Hannah, and Louisa

—J. S.

First paperback edition 2013
Text copyright © 2009 by Julie Danneberg
Illustrations copyright © 2009 by John Shelley
All rights reserved, including the right of reproduction in whole or
in part in any form. Charlesbridge and colophon are registered trademarks
of Charlesbridge Publishing, Inc.

Published by Charlesbridge
85 Main Street
Watertown, MA 02472
(617) 926-0329
www.charlesbridge.com

Library of Congress Cataloging-in-Publication Data
Danneberg, Julie, 1958–
    Family reminders / Julie Danneberg ; illustrated by John Shelley.
        p. cm.
    Summary: In 1890s Cripple Creek, Colorado, when young Mary McHugh's
father loses his leg in a mining accident, she tries to help, both by earning
money and by encouraging her father to go back to carving wooden figurines
and playing piano.
    ISBN 978-1-58089-320-6 (reinforced for library use)
    ISBN 978-1-58089-321-3 (paperback)
    [1. Family life—Colorado—Fiction. 2. Wood carving—Fiction. 3. Amputees—Fiction.
4. People with disabilities—Fiction. 5. Depression, Mental—Fiction. 6. Cripple
Creek (Colo.)—History—19th century—Fiction.] I. Shelley, John, 1959– ill. II. Title.
PZ7.D2327 Fam 2009
[Fic]—dc22   2008049659

Printed in the United States of America
(hc) 10 9 8 7 6 5 4 3 2 1
(sc) 10 9 8 7 6 5 4 3 2 1

Illustrations done in India ink and a Gillot 303 nib pen on fine-grain paper
Display type and text type set in Letterhead Fancy and ITC Legacy Serif
Color separations by Chroma Graphics, Singapore
Printed and bound December 2012 by Worzalla Publishing Company in
    Stevens Point, Wisconsin, USA
Production supervision by Brian G. Walker
Designed by Diane M. Earley

Family Reminders

Prologue

"It's going to be a warm one, Mary. *An Indian summer day," Daddy said to me as he got up from the kitchen table and slugged down his last gulp of coffee. He grabbed his lunch pail off the counter and handed me mine.*

Mama walked us both to the door. "Be careful with that," she said to Daddy, pointing to his lunch pail. "There's a piece of Mary's apple pie in there, so don't go swinging it all around when you walk to work."

"That pie was so good at dinner last night that I dreamed about it after I went to sleep," Daddy said, winking at me as he gave Mama a quick kiss and a tight hug. He put on his hat and coat and lit out the front door, taking the steps two at a time and whistling "Danny Boy" as he went.

"Wait for me," I called after him as I scrambled to catch up. Daddy was fast, but he always waited for me at the front gate.

"Have a good day," Mama called out after us as she stood on the front porch sipping her coffee and taking in the bright Colorado morning. The sun in the unclouded sky promised a perfect day. The last days of autumn were my favorite. Extra special, like the last bite of Mama's double-fudge chocolate cake. It was a beautiful mountain morning all right, and I enjoyed it just a bit more because I knew that the next day might bring the snow and cold that would last until spring.

Daddy and I walked and talked our way down the hill toward Bennett Avenue, Cripple Creek's main street. We walked past Brown's Emporium, full of fancy fripperies,

then past the grocery store and the post office. That's where we parted ways. Daddy kept going straight to the train station to catch the trolley to his job at the Irish Rose Mine. I turned right, heading uphill again. I closed my eyes as I walked past the painted-ladies house, not wanting to get a glimpse of something, or someone, I shouldn't. I trudged up a road as steep as a mountain (because it was a mountain) and called out greetings to my friends waiting in the school yard.

As the sun streamed in through the smudged schoolhouse windows, the morning passed quickly, filled with a reading lesson, a spelling test, and a page of penmanship practice.

At lunch recess I jumped rope. The smell of pine whirled around me. Dynamite blasts rumbled from deep inside the mine straight across the valley, while the twelve o'clock train hooted and hissed as it chugged around the last curve and into the station. Every once in a while, an ornery donkey hee-hawed its stubbornness.

Why do I remember this day so well? Because it was the last perfect day. I was ten years old, and I still believed that life would always roll along easy and uncomplicated.

When I daydream about that last perfect day, when I piece together all of the memories into a beautiful, sunny, sparkling picture, I always stop remembering just before the disaster siren from the mine screamed out its warning. I always stop remembering just before everything changed.

One

The mine's shrill disaster siren ripped through the everyday noises of the playground. Silence settled on the valley as the mine's dynamite blasting ceased and the clanging, stomping ore press went still. All of us on the playground stopped what we were doing. Shielding our eyes against the sun's brightness, we looked toward the telltale pile of orange-gold tailings that spilled down the mountainside away from the gold mine's tunneled entrance. We looked hard, carefully scanning the area, hoping to see something that would explain that screeching siren. But we were too far away. Besides, we all knew that the danger was inside the mountain, not outside.

My stomach lurched as I thought of Daddy inside that mountain. Usually I liked glancing across the valley, knowing that he was right there, busy at work. "Like a worker ant in an anthill," he often joked. But that day the mountain didn't seem friendly and forgiving: it loomed threatening and angry against the skyline.

My friend Emily came to stand beside me. She squeezed my hand and said, "Don't worry, Mary. I'm sure he's okay." Emily's father worked the night shift so she was spared the worry. "You know it always works out," she said. I nodded, but in my head I knew that it hadn't worked out for Matthew and Aaron O'Malley. A day after the siren went off last year, we found out that they were fatherless. Their daddy and uncle lay buried under a pile of

rocks. A week after the siren went off, there was a double funeral, and two weeks later the remaining O'Malleys moved away.

As the siren blurted out its bad news over and over and over again, I scanned the pale, scared faces of my classmates and wondered, *Is it your uncle? Is it your brother?* I didn't let myself put words to the real question that was rolling through my mind. *Is it my father?*

Finally the siren stopped. After a few minutes of silence, Miss Sullivan, white-faced and teary-eyed, gathered us up and ushered us back into school. "Let's try to keep busy, shall we?" she said as she started us on our regular afternoon lessons. Although we all went obediently through the motions, no one had thoughts of anything but what was happening in the mine across the valley.

Finally it was time to go home. Miss Sullivan helped us with our coats and sent us quickly out the door. I didn't even bother waiting for my friends. Instead I flew down the hill toward home, my feet

9

pounding the wooden sidewalk. When I reached my own block I slowed down, not wanting to rush into any bad news that might be waiting for me.

Deliberately, I opened the gate. Deliberately— one, two, three, four—I climbed the steps of the porch. I paused for a minute at the front door, took a deep breath, and walked inside.

TWO

"Is it Daddy?" I called out before the door even slammed behind me. There was no answer, but I didn't need one. There in the unlit kitchen was Mama, sitting motionless in a straight-backed chair, her hands grasped together in a white-knuckled grip in her lap, her eyes closed. My words startled them opened. I noticed they were red-rimmed.

"Is it Daddy?" I asked again, dropping my book bag to the floor and rushing to her side.

"There was an accident at the mine, Mary. Daddy was badly hurt," Mama began, speaking slowly, as if saying it that way made it somehow easier to take in, to understand. "A boulder fell on his leg. It came loose during last night's blasting and then—"

"But he's going to be okay, isn't he?" I interrupted.

"I won't know more than that until I see him and talk to the doctors." Mama punctuated the last word with a jagged breath. For the first time she reached out to touch my hand. "Aunt Hattie's coming to stay with you, and Uncle William will take me to the hospital."

"I'll go with you," I said.

Mama shook her head.

"I want to see Daddy, too. Please, Mama. Please let me come," I pleaded.

"I wish I could, Mary, but it's going to be a long night. Who knows what will happen? I don't want to be worrying about you as well as Daddy. It's best for both of us if you stay here." Mama pulled me into the cradle of her arms and rocked me like the little girl I hadn't been for a long time.

We sat there like that for a few minutes, lost in our own fears, until a knock at the door brought us both to our feet.

Aunt Hattie, Daddy's big sister, came in, fluttery and pale faced. "Don't you worry about a thing, Liddie. Mary and I will be fine until you get back."

"Thank you, Hattie," Mama said, heading toward the parlor. She pinned on her hat and slipped into her coat. I noticed her threadbare overnight bag tucked in beside the chair.

"Please, Mama, can't I come?" I asked again.

Mama said nothing, just kissed the top of my head and went out into the slanting late-afternoon light, pulling the front door shut, oh so carefully, behind her.

After Mama left I curled up on the prickly sofa and watched Aunt Hattie bustle around, trying with her busyness to put things right. She plumped cushions and straightened Daddy's piano music. She dusted the side tables and swept the floor and then rearranged the knickknacks above the fireplace, lining them up in a perfect row. Finally, she closed the heavy brocade curtains.

"Time to start dinner," she said with forced cheerfulness, making her way out of the parlor.

"Mama always leaves the drapes open," I said quietly to her retreating figure. Lying there in the dark, I remembered last Sunday afternoon when Mama came home from visiting a friend to find the drapes closed tight to the autumn sun.

"I might as well be a miner," Mama teased Daddy as she whisked the drapes open to the light.

"Now who in their right mind would want to be that?" Daddy asked with a smile, pulling her to him and swinging her off her feet.

"My point exactly," Mama sassed right back.

Mama's laughter rang out sweet and clear, while Daddy's was low and grumbly and sounded as if it bubbled up from the very tips of his toes.

Aunt Hattie's call to help startled me back to the present. "Coming," I called as I got myself up from the sofa and slowly crossed the room. Before I left the parlor, I pulled open the drapes to the last shreds of afternoon light. Standing in the warm puddle of sunshine, I felt a cold knowing grow inside me.

That night I didn't feel like eating, even when Aunt Hattie offered me the leftover pie. Aunt Hattie clucked disapprovingly, saying, "You haven't eaten a thing, Mary." I shrugged and pushed away my plate. No food would go down past the big lump in my throat.

After the dishes were washed, dried, and put away, I kissed Aunt Hattie good night and went to my room. Plopping down onto my bed, I closed my eyes for a minute, but the thoughts racing through my head forced them back open. I didn't want to think of Daddy lying in a hospital bed. I'd never been in the hospital, but from the outside it seemed scary. Its tall, brick walls made it look like a fortress, and behind those strong walls lay the weak and the sick.

I turned on my side and reached over to pick up a small, carved wooden figurine from my nightstand. It stood about six inches tall and barely fit into my hand. It was one of many that Daddy had carved for our family. He called them his Reminders. This Reminder was one of my favorites. It was a carved likeness of Mama and Daddy on their wedding day. Daddy stood soldier straight in his best suit, his arm tight around Mama's shoulder, pulling her snug in beside him.

"We're a perfect fit," Daddy said every single time he looked at the carving. "A perfect fit."

I studied the Wedding Reminder, turning it over in my hand. Mama and Daddy looked so happy and so strong. "Ready to face the world," Mama always said.

"Daddy, why do you spend so much time carving the Reminders?" I asked one day as I sat with him on the porch, watching him carefully shape each tiny detail.

"Because when I work on them they remind me of good times. It's like having a memory you can touch . . . or tickle!" he said, putting down the wood and his carving knife before he chased me, growling and laughing, down the steps and around the house. Daddy was never serious for long.

For the first time since hearing about the accident, I began to cry.

Three

I woke up the next morning to the smell of bacon sizzling and coffee brewing. For the briefest of moments it felt like any other day. All too soon, though, the memory of Daddy's injury came rushing back, and its heavy weight settled into a twisted knot at the bottom of my stomach.

"Is Mama home?" I asked Aunt Hattie as I walked into the kitchen, still in my pajamas and grateful that it was Saturday so I didn't have to worry about school and the endless questions that surely awaited me.

"No," Aunt Hattie said, "but she sent a telegram first thing this morning. Suppose she didn't want you to worry. Seems to me she better start counting each and every penny, considering the news. . . ." Her voice trailed off as she pointed to the telegram with a nod of her head, her hands covered with biscuit dough.

I picked up the thin yellow and black piece of paper. I'd never gotten a telegram before. I'd never even held one. I carried it into the parlor and folded myself into Mama's rocking chair, where I carefully flattened and smoothed the telegram against my lap.

DADDY WILL BE ALL RIGHT THE DRS COULD NOT SAVE HIS LEG I WILL BE HOME TOMORROW

The rocker squeaked as I rocked back and forth and tried to take in the news. *Daddy will be all right. Daddy will be all right.* I said Mama's words over and over again in my head, and as I did I felt a wave of relief wash over me as tears burned my eyes.

I even smiled slightly to myself as I thought about how Mama would never have allowed me to be here in the parlor first thing in the morning. The parlor was for company and for family evenings. It was definitely not for daytime use. "Might wear it out," Daddy whispered to me whenever Mama chased us out. Usually we didn't sit in here until after the evening dishes were done. Only then would Mama let us move from the hard kitchen chairs into the fireplace warmth and soft-chair comfort of the parlor. Sometimes, though, Daddy grew tired of waiting for our after-dinner family time.

"How about some music?" he asked. Swooping into the kitchen, he dragged Mama and me away from the sink, our hands still dripping with soapsuds.

"Daniel, please!" Mama laughed, wiping her hands on her apron and shaking her head. "I suppose you think the dishes will do themselves."

"I'll help you with them later," Daddy said as he escorted Mama and me into the parlor. Then he pulled the comfy chairs up to the fireplace and seated each of us with a bow. Finally, once we were settled, he took his seat at the piano and began to play. Polka music, Irish jigs—anything with a fast, toe-tapping beat. Pretty soon, as the music got under his skin, he couldn't sit any longer. Still playing, he stood up, the piano stool pushed out of the way. "Piano dancing," Daddy always called it.

22

"Plumb foolery," Mama always responded.

Whatever they called it, whenever Daddy got to his feet you could be sure that Mama and I were laughing and clapping and singing along.

The banging of pots and pans brought me back to the telegram and the news about Daddy. Staring at the silent piano, I tried to picture Daddy piano dancing on one leg.

Four

Daddy came home exactly one week and two days later. Since he'd been gone, a winter storm had blown through the valley, stripping the branches of their color and leaving a new landscape, white and bare.

Mama went to the hospital to bring him home. I stayed behind, not wanting my first sight of him to be in front of strangers. I hadn't seen him since the accident.

"No visitors," said the doctors at first.

"No visitors," Daddy said later.

"Don't expect things to be the same," Mama warned me before she left the house that morning. During the long wait I baked Daddy an apple pie. While it was in the oven, I set the table with the company tablecloth and the good china. I even ran outside and gathered pine branches to place in the big red pitcher that always sat in the center of the kitchen table. *Daddy's coming home*, I sang to myself as I prettied up the house. Daddy liked a celebration, and this would be the biggest one of all.

I heard him coming before I saw him. First I heard the squeak of the front gate as it opened, and the metal clang as it closed. I waited for his whistled hello, the one he did when he knew I was inside waiting for him. The one he always did just before he bounded up the steps, racing to beat me to the front door.

Today there was no whistle, and there were no quick footsteps up the stairs. My heart fell until I remembered Mama's warning. This was what she'd meant when she said everything was going to be different. Of course Daddy wouldn't come flying up the stairs. Mama had warned me that he was on crutches, with his leg fatly wrapped in bandages. There was no hello, only the heavy thud of crutches and then the heavier, slower sound of his good foot hitting the floor one step at a time.

When Daddy reached the porch, I ran to the front door and swung it open, knowing that he would be waiting for my welcome with arms outstretched. Instead he stood there thin and weak, clinging to his crutches.

"Daddy," I said, expecting his ready smile and loud laugh to erase the stranger in front of me. He looked at me and looked down shyly, like a little boy caught doing something wrong.

"Daddy?"

"It's been a long day, Mary. Your father is very tired right now." Mama's matter-of-fact voice cut into the awkwardness. "He insisted on walking

home from the train station. Can you imagine, in this slippery snow? We're lucky we saw Mr. Morgan's delivery wagon and he took pity on us, or we'd still be at it."

Daddy winced at the mention of needing a ride. "Pity is right. I could see the way he looked at me. Felt sorry for me, that's what."

"Of course he felt sorry for you, Daniel. You've been hurt. You're in pain. What kind of friend would he be if he didn't feel sorry for you?" Mama answered, sounding like she had already had this conversation before.

"I don't need other people's pity, Liddie. I don't want people treating me like I'm some kind of cripple."

"Mary, why don't you get your father a cup of tea?" Mama said, changing the subject. Her tired eyes and lined face contradicted her cheerful voice. "Won't that be nice, Daniel? Let's go sit down in the kitchen and warm up."

"I think I'll just go to bed," Daddy answered. He pushed past me without even looking up. The sound of his crutches scraping against the floor echoed through the house.

That night Daddy didn't come to dinner. My apple pie stayed uneaten on the table. Mama quietly folded up the tablecloth and put it away. To me, the house felt emptier than it had when Daddy was in the hospital.

Five

The wind whistled through the trees, bleak and sharp, as winter settled itself firmly onto the mountain. The autumn sounds changed to muffled winter sounds, and people stayed in their houses rather than tussle with the bitter cold and snow. The weeks passed. I kept expecting life to revert to normal. I expected Daddy's old self to return, and I expected to see Mama's face relax into an unforced smile. Instead, it seemed that nothing changed and each day felt sadder than the next.

At first Daddy spent a lot of time resting. "He's still weak from the operation," Mama explained every day when I barged in after school only to be hushed quiet because Daddy was sleeping. Again.

When he wasn't in bed, he sat listlessly at the kitchen table.

"Eat, Daniel," Mama begged, pushing food toward him. "It will make you stronger."

"For what?" Daddy said angrily, stabbing the fork into his mashed potatoes.

For us, I wanted to yell back at him. *For me*. I didn't say a word, though. I just pushed my chair noisily back from the table and, with a shake of my head, marched out of the room.

One day I walked in from school as Aunt Hattie and Mama were having a hushed conversation in

the parlor while Daddy took his afternoon nap. Bent over their words, they were too busy to notice me, so I hung my coat up and stood quietly at the door. I heard Aunt Hattie offering Mama money.

"Now, Hattie, you know that Daniel won't take charity," Mama said. "Even from his favorite sister," she added, trying to muster up a smile.

"This isn't charity, Liddie. We're family," Hattie insisted, trying to press the money into Mama's hand.

"Charity is charity, no matter where it comes from," Mama said firmly. "This family has made it through rough times before. We'll make it through this." Mama reached over and patted Aunt Hattie's hand. "Don't worry about us. We'll be all right, won't we, Mary?" Mama's look told me that she had seen me standing there all along.

As I came to stand beside her, I nodded my agreement, but inside my heart pounded and my mind raced. When I had asked about money earlier, Mama had explained that Daddy got a check from the mine because of the accident. It had never occurred to me that it might not be enough.

After Aunt Hattie left, Mama gave me a quick hug. "Don't tell your father about this," she said. "It would just make him angry."

I pulled away from her hug. "Do we need money, Mama?" I asked.

"Don't worry, we'll be fine," Mama answered, sounding just as she had with Aunt Hattie.

I searched her eyes for the truth.

Mama stood her ground. "Scoot," she said, pushing me toward my bedroom. "Seems to me you'll do anything to avoid your homework, young lady." Later though, when I walked into the kitchen to get a glass of milk, I found Mama sitting at the kitchen table with her head in her hands.

"Can't I help?" I asked, sitting down beside her. "You can have my birthday money. Or I could get a job."

Mama hugged me tight. "Thank you, Mary. But I meant it when I said not to worry. Daddy and I will figure out a way to get through this. It's not your problem."

Why isn't it my problem? Aren't I part of this family, too? I wanted to yell at Mama, but she looked so sad and tired that I couldn't. Instead I choked back my words and returned her hug.

That night, as I was getting ready for bed, I picked up one of the Reminders from my dresser. Baby Reminder. That's what Daddy had named this one. It was a likeness of my family on the day

I was christened. Mama was holding me in her lap. Daddy stood behind, his arms a protective circle around us both.

I traced the smooth fold of Mama's long dress and admired the way her gown cascaded down to the floor. I noticed Daddy's smiling face and the way both of his feet were planted so firmly on the ground. Mostly I noticed the way their arms formed a double circle around me: Mama's first, and Daddy's over hers.

As I looked at the Baby Reminder, I wished with my whole heart that our family could be that way again.

The next day I went down the street and talked to Mrs. Egan, Mrs. Martin, and Mrs. Swanson. "Of course I'll be happy to call you the next time I need a babysitter," they all said, one after the other.

By the end of that week, I had my first job.

Mama pretended I was earning fun money, and I pretended I wasn't worried. Whatever I made I stuck into the money jar on top of the refrigerator. Mama never mentioned it, but she never told me to stop, either.

Six

Months passed. The piano sat silently in the parlor, and Daddy sat silently in the kitchen. Spring slowly pushed its way into the valley, while winter still clung tightly to the mountain, refusing to release its snowy grasp.

Bit by bit Daddy recovered his strength. He moved restlessly around the house, limping from the kitchen to the bedroom to the parlor and back to the kitchen again.

One evening, after he had passed my bedroom for the third time, I followed him back into the kitchen. "Why don't you carve something?" I asked. I pulled his tools out from the top drawer of the hutch and plunked a piece of winter-hardened pine from the wood box beside the stove.

Daddy fiddled with the knife for a minute and then set it down. "I can't," he said.

"Daniel," Mama said, looking up from her ironing, "a new bookshelf in the parlor would be nice. Why don't I have Mr. Miller send over some wood?"

Daddy shook his head. "I can't, Liddie. Let's just leave it at that."

Mama didn't answer, but her mouth was set in a tight, straight line as she left the room.

But I didn't leave the room. Not this time. This time I had to say something. I knew that Daddy was hurt and unhappy. Didn't he know that I was hurt and unhappy, too?

"Why can't you?" I pushed a little harder. "Your hand isn't hurt. Your leg is getting better. You haven't even tried. How do you know you can't?" I asked, trying unsuccessfully to hold back the tears.

Daddy didn't answer. He just shrugged and looked away, defeated.

That night I went to bed without saying a word. I guess I felt defeated, too.

When Mama came in to say good night, I just turned toward the wall. Why didn't she speak up to Daddy? Why didn't she make him try?

When I came home from school the next day, Daddy was sitting at the kitchen table, a pile of curly, yellow wood shavings at his feet and in his lap. His dark head hunched over the wood as he coaxed a carving into life.

Mama shrugged when I looked at her questioningly. "He must have gotten bored with his

orneriness," she said. Although Daddy didn't re-
spond, I saw the corners of his mouth turn up.
Just a tiny bit. And a new feeling, a spring feeling,
lifted my spirits just a tiny bit, too.

After that Daddy's hands were always busy. He made the bookshelf for the parlor. He worked on a new bench for the front porch, and he also began carving new Reminders. Mama didn't mind the mess. "I just work around it," she whispered to me one afternoon as we were fixing dinner.

I didn't mind the mess, either. I loved to sit beside Daddy at the kitchen table while he worked. It was like magic to watch him uncover the secret hidden in the wood. His hands were strong and sure as he held the carving knife.

Mostly Daddy's Reminders were images from the past, from before the accident. Daddy carved a figure of our prospector friend Mr. Shay, his pack mule loaded to overflowing with supplies, mining pan, and ax. He carved Uncle William fishing. He carved a tiny stagecoach like the one that used to come to town before the railroad, and he carved a Reminder of the bear that had chased him out of the woods three summers before. In that Reminder the bear was on its hind legs and Daddy was running, every muscle straining to get away.

As the spring won its battle for the mountain and the snow began to melt, the shelf that Daddy made for the parlor became crowded with his Reminders.

Seven

The blooming branches danced in the wind and tickled the windowpane as I lay in bed and listened to Mama and Daddy's angry voices. My room was dark and cold, but it sounded colder in the kitchen. I stayed where I was, my fingers tracing the flowers Daddy had carved into my wooden headboard, remembering Sundays before the accident.

"Where are my girls?" Daddy's voice boomed through the house. Up and ready early, he tried good-naturedly to rush us through the morning and out the door. He shifted impatiently from one foot to the other, trying to hurry us both along. "You two are slower than molasses in January," he complained. But he always smiled at me when I joined him in the kitchen, and he always greeted Mama with a kiss and a compliment.

Finally hunger pushed me out of bed. When I walked into the kitchen, the angry voices stopped. Daddy was sitting at the table, working on a carving, while Mama stood at the stove.

"Morning, Daddy," I said, giving him my tightest hug. I breathed in the scent of soap and sawdust. Since the accident Daddy's smell had changed. No longer did the smell of raw earth mingle with the soap.

"Morning, Mary," he said, hugging me back.

"Morning, Mama."

"I was wondering when you were going to get yourself out of bed," she said, leaning over to give me a kiss. "Sit down. Breakfast is ready. Show Mary what you're carving, Daniel."

"Now, Liddie, don't go trying to change the subject," Daddy said, sounding exasperated. "I mean it when I say that I don't want you taking in laundry. You have enough work to do around here now that you're doing my share of the chores as well as your own. You don't need to be doing Mr. Stewart's work as well."

"Oh, fiddle, Daniel. I'm doing laundry anyway. Besides, poor Mr. Stewart is an old man and needs the help," Mama said, pouring Daddy more coffee.

"Well, I don't like it, and I don't want you to do it."

"Daniel, you listen to me," Mama said as she sat down beside him. Her voice was quiet. "I'm tired of sitting around here worrying. Worrying about money and waiting for things to change;

that's all I seem to do lately. I mean to do what I can until you're back on your feet again."

Daddy brooded for a minute. I saw his jaw clench and unclench. Then he stood, reaching unsteadily for his crutches. "Don't you mean *foot*, Liddie?" he said. The low hush of his anger trailed behind him as he hobbled out of the kitchen.

"That man is as stubborn as a mule," Mama said to me as she dished up the oatmeal into my bowl.

"Can I help you with the laundry, Mama?" I asked.

"You have school, Mary."

"But, Mama, I can help before school. Or after. I can help with the ironing. Or getting the wood."

Mama didn't look convinced. "I don't know, Mary," she said uncertainly.

"Mama, I'm tired of worrying and waiting, too. Please let me help."

Mama laughed. "You're worse than your daddy for stubbornness, that's for sure."

"I heard that," Daddy said from his bedroom.

And then we all laughed. It felt good.

47

Eight

Even before the accident, Wednesday was always wash day.

Before the sun was up, I awoke to the sound of Daddy singing as he hauled in the big steel washtub.

"Women's work is harder than mining," he joked as he brought in the last load of wood. He liked helping Mama around the house. "Makes me feel useful," he told *me as we sat down to our breakfast and watched Mama bustle around the kitchen.*

"For once," Mama teased him, dishing him up a second bowl of oatmeal.

Now Daddy stood helplessly by and watched Mama and me lug the tub in. He directed us as to where it should go in the center of the kitchen until Mama shooed him out of the way. "Daniel, I've been doing laundry all these years without your help. I'm capable of carrying on without interference!"

Daddy snatched up his carving knife and a piece of wood. "What am I supposed to do when you're working?" he asked as he hobbled angrily out of the room.

"Well, since you asked, a little music might help things along," Mama answered. She began heating up water on the stove. I trudged back and forth to the woodpile in the still, gray morning.

"Just one more load should do it," Mama said as I placed yet another armful into the wood box.

Mr. Stewart had already stopped by with his dirty clothes. Just before I left for school, Mama put a pair of his red, sagging long johns into the tub to soak.

Giggling at the sight, I said, "Looks like he really does need your help."

Mama laughed, too. "Off with you now. Mr. Stewart's underclothes are no concern of yours," she said as she stirred the clothes into the soapy water with her long-handled paddle.

I hated to leave the steamy warmth of the kitchen. Mama looked happy as she bent over the washboard, her sleeves pushed up, her arms up to her elbows in soapsuds. She was humming to herself as I let myself out the door.

The folded clothes were ready in a wicker basket by the front door when Mr. Stewart came by on his way home from work. He was accompanied by another miner, Mr. O'Brien, who had a basket of dirty clothes and a question in his eyes. Mama laughed and said yes, she could have the clothes done by tomorrow, and would this be a regular job. They shook hands when he said yes.

I peeked around the kitchen door as Mr. O'Brien left and Mr. Stewart stepped up to claim his long johns. Mr. Stewart had come to America to find his fortune. After crisscrossing the mountains, following one gold strike after another, he ended up in Cripple Creek. "Mighty obliged to you, ma'am," he said shyly. "Between working all day, cooking dinner, and trying to keep the house livable, this old bachelor just plain don't have time for anything else." As he talked he pressed a crinkled dollar into Mama's hand. Then he bowed slightly and backed out the door.

Mama called me into the parlor. "Look at this," she squealed. "One dollar! My goodness!" Mama let out a long whistle and picked up the hem of her skirt, dancing a jig.

Daddy clumped in from the kitchen and stood there, leaning on his crutches and watching Mama dance. "What's going on here?" he finally asked.

"Well, for starters, Daniel," Mama said pointedly, "I'm dancing in the parlor without any music."

Daddy just shrugged.

Mama looked at him for a moment, a challenge flashing in her eyes. "For another, I'm happy because Mr. Stewart paid me one whole dollar for doing his laundry. And I already have another job for tomorrow. See, I can help out until you get back on . . . until you get better."

"Don't you understand, Liddie? I'm not going to get better. I'm always going to be missing a leg. Let's face it, nobody's going to hire a one-legged miner."

Mama's smile faded against the rough truth of Daddy's words. Then in carefully woven words, as soft as flannel, she said, "Daniel, you're right, no one is going to hire a one-legged miner . . . to mine. But don't you understand that you are

53

more than a miner, one-legged or two? Or at least I always thought so."

She reached up to hug him, but Daddy, stiff and unbendable, held on tightly to his crutches, eyes straight ahead. Mama shook him gently by the shoulders and kissed him on the cheek. Then, putting her money in her apron pocket and her chin in the air, she flounced out of the room.

Daddy came over to me where I sat on the sofa. Smiling weakly, he dropped a Reminder in my lap. It was a carving of a woman bent over a washboard, her sleeves rolled up and her hair falling down around her face.

"It looks just like Mama," I said as I inspected it, turning it round and round.

Daddy nodded and limped slowly out of the room.

Before I followed him into the kitchen I put the carving carefully on the shelf with all the other Reminders.

Nine

"**Would you run down** to Brown's Emporium for me?" Mama asked as soon as I walked in from school and dropped my book bag on the kitchen chair.

"Oh, Mama, can't I do it tomorrow?" I asked, breathing in the delicious, warm smell of just-baked bread.

"No. Daddy is out of pipe tobacco," Mama said in a tone that made it perfectly clear that there was to be no argument. She handed me a piece of bread slathered with wild raspberry preserves. "Here, have a snack before you go," she said, softening her voice and kissing me on the head as she went back to her chores. One sweet-sour bite brought the memories of last summer flooding back.

Mama, Daddy, and I left the house early one morning to pick raspberries. We hiked up the road past the house until it was no longer a road but a dusty trail into the mountains. Daddy whistled as he carried the picnic basket and his fishing pole. Mama and I both carried tin buckets. Up and over the ridge we climbed until we reached a scraggly mountain meadow dotted with wildflowers. The creek bubbled and rushed along past the raspberry bushes, their branches full of knobby, red fruit.

"Heaven on earth," Daddy said, taking in a deep breath. I breathed in, too, big gulps of moist air that smelled of the river, pine, and the sweetness of ripe fruit.

Mama and I rolled up our sleeves and went to work plucking ripe, plump raspberries off the prickly branches.

Daddy gathered firewood and started a campfire. Then he stuck a worm on his hook and began to fish. The sun climbed higher and hotter in the sky, and the only sounds were the rustle of the raspberry branches and the rushing of the river.

Finally Daddy called us to a lunch of trout cooked over the campfire. "Why is it that food always tastes better on a picnic?" Mama asked, after cutting into the tender trout with her fork, washing it down with the icy

stream water, and topping her meal off with fresh, sweet raspberries.

"It must be my cooking," Daddy said, with a wink.

After lunch Mama stretched out on a blanket in the shade and read her book. Daddy leaned against a tree, pulled out his knife, and began to whittle, and I waded in the river. So the afternoon passed until dark thunderstorms rumbled down from the peaks and chased us home.

That night when I climbed into bed, tired and content with my day, I found the carving Daddy had been working on tucked under my pillow. It was a girl with the hem of her long skirt tucked into her waistband and an overflowing bucket of raspberries in her hand.

"Hurry up, Mary. It will be dark soon," Mama said, her voice rousing me from my reverie. "Here's a dime. Tell Mr. Brown that Daddy needs more pipe tobacco. He'll know which kind."

"Just one minute, Mama," I said as I ducked quickly into my room and grabbed the Raspberry

Reminder still sitting on my dresser. It was a good memory, and I wasn't ready to leave it behind. I stuck the Reminder into my coat pocket and headed out the door and down the hill toward Bennett Avenue.

Ten

The bell at the top of the door jingled, and a voice from the back said, "I'll be out in just a minute."

"That's okay, Mr. Brown," I called back. "Don't hurry. It's just me, Mary McHugh." The truth is, I was glad to have a chance to wander around the store alone, breathing in the spicy-sweet smell of tobacco. Outside, the sign read "Brown's Emporium: The Finest Things in Life." Inside, the store

was crowded with shelves and glass display cases full of beautiful things to buy: fancy marble chess sets, carved wooden pipes, delicate music boxes, jewelry, and sculptures from all around the world. As I looked around I thought about the town's rich mine managers, bankers, and store owners who bought these trinkets.

"Well, hello, Mary," Mr. Brown said as he came out of the store's back room. "What can I do for you today?"

"I came to get some more of Daddy's pipe tobacco," I said, fishing in my pocket for the dime Mama had given me earlier. "I know it's here somewhere," I said nervously. A dime was a lot of money, and our family couldn't afford to lose even a penny. I emptied the contents of my pocket out onto the counter. I pulled out a purple-veined rock that I'd found up on the mountain, Daddy's Raspberry Reminder, and a piece of hard candy. "Here it is," I said finally, holding up the dime triumphantly.

"And here is your daddy's tobacco," Mr. Brown said, looking over the treasures lined up across the counter. "This is mighty fine work," he said, picking up Daddy's carving and inspecting it with an experienced eye over the top of his glasses. "Yes, mighty fine indeed," he said softly to himself. He turned it over and over in his hand, inspecting the delicate details of the girl's dress and bucket.

"Where did you get this, Mary?" he asked at last.

"It's my Raspberry Reminder. Daddy made it for me last summer after we went raspberry picking. He carves lots of things. He even makes furniture," I boasted proudly, feeling happy that I had something to brag about.

"This is beautiful, Mary. Your daddy is a real artist," Mr. Brown said slowly. "How 'bout I buy it from you? I could easily sell it in the store."

I smiled as I pictured Daddy's Reminder sitting on the shelf in some fancy mansion up on the hill, or better yet, wrapped up and taken to Denver. "Thank you, Mr. Brown, but I can't. See, it's me.

I'm holding my pail of raspberries. I could never sell it. Especially now . . ."

Mr. Brown looked over the carving once more before giving it back. "Well, if you ever change your mind, you know where to find me."

I walked home with my hand wrapped around the smoothly carved piece of wood in my pocket and my mind wrapped around a new picture of Daddy. A real artist!

Eleven

As I trudged up the hill toward home, I watched the sun go down behind the mountain, its last rays of golden light tangled on the ragged peaks. The mine's evening whistle echoed off the mountain walls, signaling the end of the day shift. Soon a string of twinkling lights streamed forth as the miners, with headlamps still on, headed down the path toward home.

Sometimes, before the accident, Mama and I used to watch those twinkling lights as they slid down the mountain.

Which One Is Daddy? was a guessing game we played.

"*I think he's the one in the back of the line,*" Mama said. "*Probably got so tied up talking to Mr. Egan about the Saturday dance at church that he forgot to leave the mine.*"

"*I bet he's the first in line, Mama. He knows you're making roast chicken for dinner tonight. You know he's never late for your roast chicken.*"

We both laughed.

That night I sat on the top step for a few moments and once again enjoyed the cheerful sight of the strand of pearly lights. When I finally went inside, I was greeted by the welcome-home smell of Mama's dinner and Daddy's called-out hello from the kitchen. He sat in his usual place at the

table, working on a carving. I handed him his tobacco and leaned over his shoulder, watching the
knife blade bite into the wood, chewing away the
surface bit by bit.

"What are you making, Daddy?"

"Just another Reminder," he said, showing me
the figure of a man playing the piano. It was
Daddy before the accident. Even in the carving I
could see that his whole body moved to the music.

His eyes were closed, his head was thrown back, and a broad smile lit up his face.

Before the accident, Aunt Hattie and Uncle William used to tease Daddy about his playing.

"Goodness' sake, Daniel, you're acting like a wild man," Aunt Hattie said, shaking her head with disapproval.

Daddy laughed and said, "I can't help it, Hattie. I play the way I feel. And I feel happy when I play."

I thought about Daddy's piano dancing as I took the Reminder from his hand. "It looks just like you, Daddy," I said. I remembered the words Mr. Brown had used earlier. "Daddy, you are an artist, you know that?"

"Nope. Just a one-legged miner who carves," Daddy answered.

Although his words were sad, he tried to say them jokingly. It was as if he thought that talking about missing his leg would help him get used to it. This time his words didn't make me sad. They made me angry. "No, just a one-legged artist who used to mine," I fired back, daring him to see himself differently.

Daddy just laughed, his smile flashing and his eyes sparkling. He took the Reminder back from me and looked it over carefully.

"Well, I still say you are an artist, Daddy, and so does Mr. Brown. And he knows what he's talking about, so there," I said, kissing him on the cheek. "Can I have another one of the Reminders?"

"Take any that you want. Except this one," he said, putting the Piano Reminder beside him on the table. "I think I'll keep this one for myself."

Twelve

That night after dinner, we lingered at the table.

"Mary," Daddy said, "Mama and I want to talk to you about something."

Just the way he said it, slow and measured, made my heart drop. I held my breath as he began to talk.

"I've been sitting here thinking about the future, our future," Daddy said. "I'm feeling better now, and I'm getting around pretty good on my crutches."

"I know, Daddy." I smiled encouragingly.

"So, I think I'm ready to start looking for a job. What do you think about that?"

I let out my breath. "I think that's a good thing. Is that what you wanted to tell me?"

"Mary, I'm going to start looking for work here in Cripple Creek. But I don't know what kind of luck I'll have. I might have to look in Denver, too. It's a big city. There are more jobs there. More kinds of jobs that I could do. . . ."

"But I don't want to move," I said, the tears quickly welling up.

"That's how I feel, too, Mary. It's how we both feel," he said, looking at Mama for support. "But I wanted to warn you, just in case."

"But what about Aunt Hattie and Uncle William? And Mama's laundry business? And my babysitting? What about school? And church and our friends?" Inside, though, I already knew the answer to all my questions. I knew it was good that Daddy was feeling well enough to look for a job. That's what I had wanted. For all of us. Still, a tear splashed down my cheek.

"Now, Mary," Daddy said, his voice soft and gentle, "don't go expecting the worst just yet. You know I'll try my best to keep us here. I just thought you should know what we're thinking."

The next morning, Daddy surprised me by walking into the kitchen in his Sunday suit. His curly hair was wet and combed flat to his head, and a smile was plastered across his face. I couldn't help but smile back.

"Doesn't your father look handsome?" Mama asked, leaning down to give him a kiss.

I nodded my agreement. "Why are you dressed up, Daddy?" I asked.

Daddy took a hungry bite of toast and said, "I'm going to talk with the manager of the mine. I'm going to see if he can give me a job. I thought maybe they could use me in the office."

"But, Daddy, why would you want to go back to the mine? There are a lot of other things you could do," I said, remembering what Mr. Stewart had told me once about an injured miner: *"His luck has*

run out. That's why he got injured. You surely don't want
someone like that around a load of dynamite, do you?"

I knew Daddy wasn't bad luck. He wasn't. But
I also knew that he wasn't going to like the answer
they gave him at the mine.

"Mr. Brown said you are an artist, and no one
can play the piano like you. People are always
saying so." Tears burned my eyes, but I blinked
them back. More than anything, I didn't want to
see Daddy hurt again. Especially now, when he
was feeling so much better, so much happier.

Daddy's voice got firmer, and there was an
angry edge to his words. "Mary, you said you
wanted to stay here. That you didn't want to move.
Well, if we are going to stay, then I need to get a
job. Don't you understand? I need to start pulling
my weight around here."

"Now, Daniel," Mama interrupted, "no need to
get angry. Mary just wants what's best for you."

"You're right, Liddie," Daddy said, swallowing
his anger along with his coffee. "Don't worry about

me, Mary. This is what's best." He pushed himself away from the table, heaved himself up to his crutches, and clumped out of the kitchen.

"But, Mama—," I started to say as soon as he left the room.

"Hush, Mary. You know how stubborn your father is. I can't tell him what to do. He has to figure things out for himself."

But I understood better than Daddy did. He couldn't go back to the mine. They wouldn't let him. I knew that. Why didn't he?

Thirteen

When I ran home up the long, steep hill after school that afternoon, I saw Mama and Daddy sitting on the front porch. I could tell right away that something was wrong. Daddy wasn't smiling anymore. His shoulders sagged, and he seemed to shrink in on himself. He looked like he had those first few weeks after the accident.

"What's the matter?" I asked.

"I didn't get it," Daddy said, without looking up. "The mine manager took one look at my missing leg and said no. Just like that. Without any discussion. Just no." Daddy shook his head, his voice quiet. "I followed him around, practically begging him to give me a job. He wouldn't reconsider. Said that it would make the other miners too nervous to see me without my leg."

"But, Daniel," Mama interrupted, "maybe you can go back later. . . ."

"I can't go back," Daddy said firmly. "I know that now. I can never go back."

Mama's eyes filled with tears, and her forehead creased with worry. "This is just your first day of looking. You know you'll find a job eventually."

"I don't know anything of the sort, Liddie. That's just the problem. What if everyone feels the way they do at the mine? What then, Liddie?"

Mama shook her head. "We can move to Denver. Surely you can find work there," Mama said, sounding as sad as Daddy.

After that Daddy didn't go out anymore to look for a job. Instead, he settled back into his old routine of wandering aimlessly around the house. When he did sit down, it was with his hands folded and still in his lap and his mind far away. We ate dinner in silence, and as soon as we were done, Daddy took himself off to bed. Although late spring was warming up the valley, our house felt as cold as a winter snowstorm.

78

For the first few days I ignored Daddy's sadness, thinking that it would go away. But it didn't, and instead of feeling sorry for him, like I did right after the accident, I was angry. Really, really angry.

One evening as we were finishing up the last bit of Mama's double-fudge chocolate cake, I caught Daddy off guard just as he was about to leave the table. I don't know if I wanted to start a fight or just push him to talk, but I asked him defiantly, "Daddy, why don't you play the piano anymore?"

Mama shot me a warning look from across the table, but I pretended not to see. Daddy looked surprised at the directness of the question.

"Well, I'm not exactly sure," he said, shifting uncomfortably in his chair. After a pause he added softly, "I guess I feel like there isn't any music left inside of me, Mary."

"But, Daddy, don't you remember how you told Aunt Hattie that the music came from your heart? Your heart hasn't changed, has it?"

Daddy didn't answer. I looked over and saw Mama bending intently over her plate, her lips quivering.

After a while I had an answer for him. "Well, Daddy, my heart hasn't changed and neither has Mama's. We're still both here, missing you. Missing you and wishing you would come back to us. And I'm getting tired of waiting." And before Daddy could leave us behind again, I got up and walked out of the room.

Fourteen

After school the next day, I headed straight for Brown's Emporium. When the bell on top of the door jingled, Mr. Brown looked up from his paper. "Well, hello, Mary. Don't tell me that your daddy needs more tobacco?"

"No. I came because I have some business to discuss with you, Mr. Brown," I answered, trying to sound as grown-up as possible.

Mr. Brown's eyes widened in surprise. "This sounds serious, Mary. Why don't we step into my office?" He motioned to the back of the store.

I followed him back. I had never been in his office before. It looked just like Mr. Brown—worn and comfortable. He pulled out a chair for me before seating himself in the cracked leather chair behind his desk. Leaning back, his hands folded across his large stomach, he said, "Well, young lady, what can I do for you?"

I gathered my thoughts for a minute, and then I said, "Mr. Brown, you said that you wanted to buy the carving my daddy made of me holding the raspberry pail. Do you remember?"

"Sure I do, Mary."

"Well, I decided that I want to sell it to you. I brought a couple of other carvings that I thought you might want to buy, too." I reached into my book bag, pulled out the three bundles, and lined them up on the desk, like three presents waiting to be opened.

"My, my," Mr. Brown said under his breath as he carefully unwrapped each package and inspected the Reminder that he found inside. Meanwhile, I inspected his face, looking for a clue as to whether he liked what he saw.

After what seemed like a very long time, Mr. Brown put down the last Reminder. "These are mighty fine pieces of work, Mary. My offer still stands. I'd love to buy them, if you're sure you want to sell them."

I let out my breath in a huge sigh and nodded enthusiastically. "Yes, I'm sure," I said.

"Let me ask you this, Mary. Does your daddy know you're selling these?" he asked, peering at me gently over his glasses.

"These are *my* Reminders, Mr. Brown," I said with feeling. "Daddy gave them to me, so I figure I can do what I want with them. I definitely want to sell them."

"All right then," Mr. Brown said, slapping his knee. "You've got yourself a deal, young lady. I can

probably charge my customers six dollars for each figurine. So I think three dollars each is a fair price to offer you. Is that amount okay with you, Mary?"

"Y-y-y-y-yes," I stammered, trying to sound calm while inside my stomach was doing somersaults and flips. "Three dollars sounds just right."

Mr. Brown unlocked the safe behind his desk and pulled out a gray, metal cash box. "Let's see," he said, reaching in for the dollar bills. "That means I owe you nine dollars."

He counted out nine one-dollar bills into my open palm. When he was done and I had rolled up the money and stuck it in my pocket, he gave me a piece of paper. "Show this receipt to your daddy, Mary. Make sure to tell him that if he has any questions to come and talk to me." Mr. Brown pushed himself away from his desk and stood up. He gave a little bow. "It's been a pleasure doing business with you, young lady," he said as he reached over to shake my hand.

Together we walked out of the office into the cluttered, sweet-smelling store. I looked around, wondering where Mr. Brown would display Daddy's Reminders. Three dollars apiece! I could hardly believe it.

Right before he opened the door, Mr. Brown stopped me and said, "Mary, tell your daddy that if his carvings sell as well as I think they will, I'd love to work out a permanent business arrangement."

I nodded and smiled as I walked out the door, my empty book bag bumping against my side. Once past Mr. Brown's windows, I danced a little dance, full of excitement, full of hope, and—I stopped short—full of fear. What would Daddy say when he found out what I'd done?

Fifteen

When I got home that afternoon, I walked straight into the parlor, ignoring Daddy's sad hello. I looked over all the Reminders on the shelf. They were lined up across the mantel like a time line of Daddy's life. It surprised me to see that they were dusted, since we never used this room anymore. It stayed dark and stuffy all the time, and there was an empty space where Mama's rocker used to be.

At first, when Daddy started moving around after the accident, we tried to use the parlor in the evenings, more out of habit than anything else. But the silent piano reminded us too loudly of how everything had changed. So Mama moved her rocker and her sewing basket into a corner of the kitchen. "It's warmer by the stove," she said when I asked her why.

After that, evenings were spent in the kitchen, with both Mama and Daddy willingly adjusting to the change in our routine. For me, the change wasn't so easy to bear. *You hardly even gave it a chance,* I wanted to yell at them. But I didn't. I had already learned that for Mama and Daddy, avoiding a problem was easier than trying to fix it.

As I stood in the darkened parlor, looking over the Reminders, Daddy came limping in. "What are you doing in here?" he asked.

"I'm looking at your Reminders," I said, turning to look him straight in the eye. "I'm trying to figure out which ones to sell next."

Daddy looked puzzled.

I pulled the roll of money out of my book bag. "Here," I said. "This is for you."

"Mary McHugh," he said sternly, taking the money and looking it over. "Where on earth did you get this?"

"Mr. Brown gave it to me. I sold him some of your Reminders. Actually, I sold him three of your Reminders, and he paid me three dollars apiece."

"Oh, Mary . . . ," Mama whispered as she came into the room.

"I only sold him the ones that Daddy had already given me. I figured since they were mine, it was okay." I talked fast, hoping to outtalk Mama and Daddy's questions.

They didn't say a word, just stared at me as if that would somehow make things clear. To fill up the silence, I told them how it all started,

how Mr. Brown had asked to buy the Raspberry
Reminder.

"At first I said no, but then today I went right
in and sold it to him. Along with a couple others
that Daddy gave to me. And, Daddy, Mr. Brown
said that he wanted to set up a permanent arrangement. He said that your carvings fit in perfectly
with the other beautiful things in his store."

Mama took the pile of money from Daddy's hand. "Nine dollars, my goodness," she said, fanning the money in front of her. And then she started to smile. "Daniel, I hope you're ready to work. Seems to me that you just got a job!" I waited nervously, staring at Daddy's face, wishing he would say something.

Daddy took the money back from Mama, slowly counted it, and looking me right in the eye, started to laugh. A great big before-the-accident laugh. He laughed and shook his head and swept me up in a great big bear hug. I didn't say a word, just smiled and held on as tight as I could.

Sixteen

That night after dinner I didn't even bother asking Mama or Daddy if it was okay. I took matters into my own hands and moved Mama's rocking chair back into the parlor and lit a fire in the fireplace.

Mama sat and sewed while Daddy paced restlessly around the room. Finally she said, "For heaven's sake, Daniel, you're making me nervous. Mary, go get your daddy's carving from the kitchen." I got up to leave but stopped at the piano.

"Why don't you play something, Daddy?"

Daddy looked at me. "Hush, Mary," he said quietly. His words held no smile.

"Just try," I insisted.

"I told you, Mary," he said, "I'm not sure I can anymore."

"You won't know 'til you try," I said as I pulled out the piano stool for him to sit on.

Daddy hesitated for a moment and then leaned his crutches against the wall and sat down heavily, staring at the keys and keeping his hands clasped tightly in his lap.

Unable to remain quiet, I urged him again. "Play, Daddy. Please."

He laid his hands lightly on the keys for a moment and then played a few chords. The sound of the piano vibrated loudly through the house, strange and unfamiliar.

Don't stop, I begged him silently. *Please don't give up. Just give it a chance.*

Daddy looked at Mama, then at me. He shook out his fingers, took a deep breath, and began again. At first he played some scales. He played gently, gingerly, as if he were awakening the piano from a long sleep. Then he stopped.

"Go on, Daniel," Mama said softly. "Play 'Danny Boy.' I'd surely love to hear that again."

"If I can remember it," Daddy said, almost shyly. Slowly, hesitantly at first, with his eyes open, he played. Then gradually, warming to the lilting beauty of the piece, his eyes closed and his body swayed in time to the music.

Mama came and stood behind me to listen, her arms around my shoulders, tears streaming down her face.

The room was filled once again with Daddy's music. I think his heart was filled, too.

Daddy stopped after one song. "Don't want to wear myself out," he said, nudging me playfully and

winking at Mama. "That piano playing is a lot of work." When I watched him hobble out, I swear his step was lighter then it had been since the accident.

"It's just like it used to be," I whispered happily to Mama. Inside I knew it wasn't exactly the same. Daddy didn't piano dance and Mama had worry lines crisscrossing her forehead when she watched Daddy play. Still, it was close enough for me.

Seventeen

Daddy went in to talk to Mr. Brown the next day,
and they did set up a permanent business arrangement. Daddy's carvings sold well right from the
start, mostly to visitors who wanted to take a piece
of the West home with them. He started making
furniture, too, like the bed he had carved for me
and the bookshelf he had made for Mama. Soon
he had more work than he had time. He spent

much of the day busy in the kitchen or, if the weather was nice, on the front porch, lost in carving. One afternoon as I sat beside him, I remembered another afternoon, from before the accident.

Daddy hadn't been to work for two days, his cough so bad that Mama finally insisted that he go to the doctor. "He'll be fine," the doctor reassured them both, "but I think it's a good idea to take a few days away from the damp and the dirt of the mountain. Just to be safe." That was all Mama needed to hear.

"I'm fine, Liddie," Daddy argued, but he was no match for Mama's stubbornness. That afternoon when I came home from school, Daddy was carving at the kitchen table. I expected him to be anxious about missing work, but he smiled up at me and showed me the Reminder he had been working on that day. It was of a man sitting on a bench, hunched over his carving. I nodded my approval as I pulled my homework out of my book bag. It was nice to have Daddy home in the afternoon. We

worked together until, in the middle of our silence, Daddy laughed out loud and said, "Mary, my girl, this is the life. Look at me, playing in the middle of the day. You'd think I was one of the rich mine owners."

"Don't go getting any of your crazy ideas," Mama said, interrupting his daydreams with common sense. And we all laughed together.

I smiled at the memory, and I smiled even more when I looked over at Daddy "playing" in the middle of the day. He was surely happy. No doubt about it. True, maybe it was a different kind of happy. Maybe it was a deeper kind of happy. Whatever it was, I was glad to see him smiling again.

One day at the end of summer, when the wildflowers had wilted and the mountain meadows were baked brown under the midday sun, Daddy came home from the doctor's with good news. "My leg is healed enough to be fitted with an artificial leg," he announced.

"A what?" I asked.

"A fake leg," Daddy answered, pulling at my hair. "That means I can finally get rid of these blasted crutches. I have to go to a special doctor in Denver, but at least now we can afford the train ticket."

Aunt Hattie came to stay with me while Mama and Daddy went to get Daddy's new leg. While they were in Denver, Mama took some of his carvings around to the fancy downtown stores. "I never would have had the courage if you hadn't done it first," she whispered to me after she got home. Although no one was as nice as Mr. Brown, the store owners recognized the quality of Daddy's work and bought everything Mama had. There were even requests for more.

The night that Mama and Daddy came home, I set the table and tried to keep busy so as not to think about the last time I waited for Daddy's return. When I heard the wagon come to a halt in front of our house, for a moment I hesitated, too nervous to hurry into a greeting that might leave me feeling empty once again. But when I passed by the new Raspberry Reminder sitting on the shelf in the parlor, I remembered all that we had already been through. I found my courage, and I pulled open the door just as Daddy let out his five-note whistled hello. I saw him standing right there in front of me, a tall man on two legs.

"Aren't you going to welcome me home?" Daddy asked.

I threw myself into his arms, hugging him tighter than tight, and whispered in his ear, "Welcome home, Daddy. Welcome home."

Author's Note

Family Reminders takes place in the late 1890s in Cripple Creek, Colorado, one of the most famous mining towns in the West. In 1900, more than eighteen million dollars worth of gold was mined from the nearly five hundred mines in the area.

The story of Mary McHugh is loosely based on the life of my grandmother, who spent part of her childhood in Cripple Creek. Her father—my great-grandfather—was a hard-rock miner who, like Daniel in the story, lost his leg in a mining accident. Although the mine where Daniel worked is fictional, my grandmother recalled the many mines that constantly belched smoke and emitted noisy blasts. Residents grew accustomed to the noise and ever-present view of mines dotting the mountainside.

Much of my description of the town is based on old photographs and research as well as on my own memories of visiting Cripple Creek as a little girl with my grandmother. Bennett Avenue was and still is the town's main street, and my grandmother's school was located up a very steep hill a few blocks off of it. At the time of this story, a trolley had been built to carry workers up and down the valley to their jobs in the mines. Mr. Brown and his store are fictional; however, in a bustling boomtown, stores like his did exist, providing access to higher-end home items that wouldn't be found in a regular department store.

You can visit Cripple Creek's official website at **www.cripple-creek.co.us** to read more about the town's mining history and see pictures of the town as it looks today.